THE
ASTRONOMICALLY
GRAND PLAN

Don't Miss Any of Astrid's
Out-of-This-World Adventures!

The Astronomically Grand Plan

The Unlucky Launch

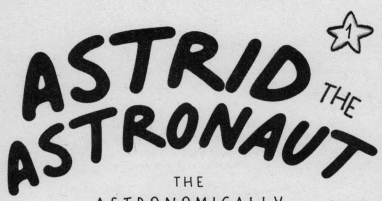

ASTRID THE ASTRONAUT

THE
ASTRONOMICALLY
GRAND PLAN

By Rie Neal ★ Illustrated by Talitha Shipman

ALADDIN

New York London Toronto Sydney New Delhi

This book is a work of fiction. Any references to historical events, real people, or real places are used fictitiously. Other names, characters, places, and events are products of the author's imagination, and any resemblance to actual events or places or persons, living or dead, is entirely coincidental.

ALADDIN • An imprint of Simon & Schuster Children's Publishing Division • 1230 Avenue of the Americas, New York, New York 10020 • First Aladdin paperback edition July 2022 • Text copyright © 2022 by Rie Neal • Illustrations copyright © 2022 by Talitha Shipman • Also available in an Aladdin hardcover edition. • All rights reserved, including the right of reproduction in whole or in part in any form. • ALADDIN and related logo are registered trademarks of Simon & Schuster, Inc. • For information about special discounts for bulk purchases, please contact Simon & Schuster Special Sales at 1-866-506-1949 or business@simonandschuster.com. • The Simon & Schuster Speakers Bureau can bring authors to your live event. For more information or to book an event contact the Simon & Schuster Speakers Bureau at 1-866-248-3049 or visit our website at www.simonspeakers.com. • Book designed by Laura Lyn DiSiena • The illustrations for this book were rendered digitally. • The text of this book was set in Ionic No 5. • Manufactured in the United States of America 0522 OFF • 2 4 6 8 10 9 7 5 3 1 • Library of Congress Cataloging-in-Publication Data • Names: Neal, Rie, author. | Shipman, Talitha, illustrator. • Title: The astronomically grand plan / by Rie Neal ; illustrated by Talitha Shipman. | Description: First Aladdin paperback edition. | New York : Aladdin, 2022. | Series: Astrid the astronaut ; book 1 | Audience: Ages 6 to 9 | Summary: Astrid is excited about her upcoming first year of Shooting Stars, a club dedicated to all things space, but now that her best friend Hallie is more interested in art Astrid is not sure her goal of becoming an astronaut will happen without her friend. • Identifiers: LCCN 2021023871 (print) | LCCN 2021023872 (ebook) | ISBN 9781534481480 (hardcover) | ISBN 9781534481473 (paperback) | ISBN 9781534481497 (ebook) • Subjects: CYAC: Friendship—Fiction. | Clubs—Fiction. | Middle schools—Fiction. | Schools—Fiction. • Classification: LCC PZ7.1.N3826 As 2022 (print) | LCC PZ7.1.N3826 (ebook) | DDC [Fic]—dc23 • LC record available at https://lccn.loc.gov/2021023871 • LC ebook record available at https://lccn.loc.gov/2021023872

FOR BRIAN, MY HUSBAND
AND BEST FRIEND
—R. N.

TO MY SISTER, WHO'S ALWAYS
HAD STARS IN HER EYES
—T. S.

CONTENTS

★ CHAPTER 1 ★

FREE "FIREWORKS"

I tapped my clock for the millionth time: 12:06 a.m.

The numbers flashed off like they always did. As if they were mad I'd woken them up.

I sat up in bed. It was so dark, it felt like I was in a black hole. Not that I'd ever been near one, of course. But I could guess.

Maybe Stella was awake too. If our room

wasn't so dark, it would make waiting easier.

As I stepped out of bed, my foot landed on a tiny, sharp thing. "Owww!" I whispered, rubbing it. Couldn't Stella keep her building bricks on *her* side? It was bad enough that her half-finished robots made weird shadows in the dark.

I peeled back the curtain, and light poured in. It lit up the stars on our ceiling and the drawing of AstroCat above my bed. The street-light was so bright, it should've woken up my big sister. But the Stella-shaped mound of blankets just rose up and down.

She used to be the one to wake *me* up for these things. But this past summer it was like she had decided she was too old for everything. She'd started middle school a week ago, and it had only gotten worse.

Better put my hearing aids in, I thought. Then I'd be all ready when our parents came to wake us up.

I opened the box next to my bed and pulled my hearing aids out. My new pair was perfect—dark blue with silver sparkles like the night sky. Last time I'd had new hearing aids, I hadn't been old enough to pick the color. But I was eight—almost nine—now. Old enough for lots of things.

Clicking my aids on, I heard the tune that meant they were starting up.

My hearing aids helped me hear better. With them, I could hear dogs bark, doors open, and people talk. I could still hear some sounds without them, but not if those sounds were quiet.

The door creaked open, and Mom's head poked in. Dad followed her.

"Astrid!" Mom gasped. "How long have you been awake?"

"Does this mean it's time?" I bounced on my toes. "Can we go up on the roof now?"

Mom smiled. "Yes."

Dad poked the lump of bedding. "Stella, are you coming?"

"Mmmf," said the lump. It flopped a pillow over its head.

Dad shrugged.

"Come on, Stella!" I pulled on her arm, but she jerked it back. "Well, fine. Be that way."

If my sister wanted to skip a family tradition, whatever. I would *never* do that when *I* was older.

"We have to go or we'll miss it!" I steered my parents out the door.

We took the elevator up to the roof deck, arms full of blankets.

Two years ago we'd lived in a big house in Arizona. We'd had our own yard, too. I missed Arizona, but our house there didn't have a roof deck. Arizona also didn't have my best friend, Hallie. So really, our condo here in California was better.

Before we'd even sat down, a light streaked across the sky.

"Look!" I cried. "The first rock!"

Dad laughed. "Most people would call them 'shooting stars,'" he said. "But no, not my daughter."

"Well, they *are* rocks," I said. "Rocks burning up when they hit Earth's atmosphere. Right?" Eyes fixed on the sky, I sat cross-legged on the deck.

"That's right, kiddo." Mom hugged me close. "We can't let you stay up too long. Big day tomorrow."

"I know," I said. "The first day of Shooting Stars."

My stomach flip-flopped. I wished that Stella was still at my school and still in Shooting Stars. But at least I'd know Hallie.

Shooting Stars was an after-school club that did space stuff. You had to be in third, fourth, or fifth grade to join, so this would be my first year. This was all part of the Astronomically Grand Plan. (It used to be called the "Grand Plan," but this past summer, I'd learned the word "astronomical." It meant "really big" and sounded space-y, too. So I added it.) One day I was going to be the first astronaut with hearing aids.

I'd taped the plan above my desk so I'd see it every day. It went like this:

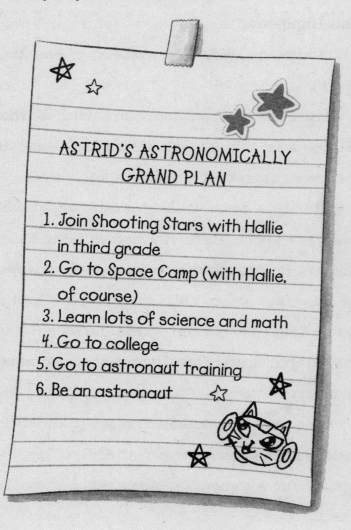

ASTRID'S ASTRONOMICALLY GRAND PLAN

1. Join Shooting Stars with Hallie in third grade
2. Go to Space Camp (with Hallie, of course)
3. Learn lots of science and math
4. Go to college
5. Go to astronaut training
6. Be an astronaut

"The Shooting Stars go to Space Camp every year," I reminded my mom. "I can't wait till Hallie and I can go next summer!" Hallie had been my best friend since we moved here two years ago. We played rocket ships on the swings. And we both loved watching *AstroCat*. Hallie could even draw her—she'd done the picture I had above my bed.

Mom kissed my head. "Only a *few* kids go each year, sweetie. Space Camp is expensive. I think it'd be better to go when you're older. You'll get more out of it."

"I know that's what you think. But—"

Behind us, the door to the roof deck creaked open. It was Stella!

She stood there, rubbing her eyes. "Did I miss the meteor shower?"

"Nope. We saved you a spot." Dad patted

the space next to him. "Free fireworks for all."

I scooted over to make room. A light shot across the sky again, sparkling like glitter.

"Ooooh," we all said.

I leaned over to my sister as she sat down. "Stella, what was your first Astro Mission? Did you have one on the first day of Shooting Stars?"

Stella yawned. "I don't remember. It was forever ago."

"Only a couple of years," I groaned. "What about Ms. Ruiz? Tell me again what she's like." Ms. Ruiz taught STEM to the older kids at our school. (STEM stood for "Science, Technology, Engineering, and Math.") She also led the Shooting Stars. Stella said she wore a flight suit a lot. And that she didn't always act like other teachers.

Mom laughed, pulling my curls back from my eyes. "Slow down, kiddo. Why don't you just try to have fun for now?"

"Mom, Shooting Stars *is* fun. So is Space Camp. And Hallie and I *really* want to go."

"Oh, I remember the plan." Mom smiled. "And I know you want to go. But again, it's expensive. Your sister has been only once."

"And I had to wait till I was eleven," Stella added.

I sighed. Stella had gone to Space Camp just two months ago. It had been a special robotics one. Now she spent all her time texting kids she'd met there. And building robots—*lots* of robots.

She'd filled our room with building bricks, motors, and circuit boards.

"Eleven?" I bit my lip.

There had to be a way to go sooner than that.

And maybe Shooting Stars could help me find it.

⋆ CHAPTER 2 ⋆

ALL ALONE

"See you tomorrow!" My new third-grade teacher, Mr. Klein, waved. Kids hurried past him, waving back. It was the first day for *all* after-school clubs, not just Shooting Stars. Everybody was in a hurry to leave.

I zipped my backpack shut. This year Mom had found one with a galaxy print. Perfect for my first year of Shooting Stars!

"Here you go, Astrid." Mr. Klein held out the clip-on mic that worked with my hearing aids. The mic made whoever wore it sound like they were right next to me. "Did it work okay?" he asked. "I'm still getting used to it."

"Yes, great," I told Mr. Klein as I slipped the mic into its pouch.

"I just met the audiologist for the school district, Miss Wong. She says you take it to the other teachers, so they can use it too. Is that right?"

Hallie was almost at the door by now. I kept trying to talk to her today, but she was always busy. At recess she'd helped Mr. Klein sort papers. At lunch she'd said she wanted to start her homework. But Hallie and I always waited for each other after school.

"What? Um . . . yes, that's right. Bye!" I

waved to Mr. Klein and hurried to the door.

I caught up with Hallie outside. "Hey," I panted. "You're going the wrong way. Shooting Stars is in the STEM lab." I pointed to the back of the school.

Hallie looked at her feet. Her shiny black hair fell over her face. "Um . . . my mom said she'd pick me up at the front of the school."

My jaw dropped. "You can't miss the first meeting!" I blurted. "I mean . . . what if there's an Astro Mission today? You'll be behind."

But she shook her head. "Astrid, um . . . I'm not doing Shooting Stars."

I blinked. "What?"

Hallie's eyes darted away. "I have to go. My . . . um . . . my mom will be here soon. Let's talk more later, okay?"

There had to be something wrong. Maybe

her parents had said no. But why wouldn't they want her in Shooting Stars?

I opened my mouth to ask, but Hallie was already gone.

☆   ☆   ☆

Other kids ran past me as I shuffled down the hall toward the STEM lab.

By myself.

Now that Stella was in middle school, I couldn't ask her for help when I was having a bad day. First Stella had left me, now Hallie.

I didn't get it. Hallie and I had been best friends for two whole years. It had been scary coming to such a big school. My school in Arizona had been a lot smaller, and there were other kids there with hearing aids. But my first day here, Hallie had worn a dress with glow-in-the-dark stars on it. She'd taught me how to draw an alien in the dirt. Right then, I knew we'd be best friends and do everything together. So I'd made the plan. We'd been looking forward to this day since we met.

As I stepped into the STEM lab, I looked around. I didn't know anybody. I mean, not really. I usually spent all my time with Hallie.

It was like I was the new kid all over again.

High tables with black tops filled most of the room. Four tall stools stood around each table. A teacher with short black hair was busy filling some paper bags at the front of the room. *Ms. Ruiz*, I realized.

I set my backpack on a table at the front. Picking at the seams, I watched the room. More kids were coming in, finding their friends. They talked and laughed.

Maybe Hallie was worried Shooting Stars

would be boring. Maybe it was like playing astronaut training on the monkey bars—I had to talk her into it, but she always had fun in the end. If I told her how great Shooting Stars was, maybe she'd change her mind.

I'd have to take good notes so I could help her catch up.

I pulled my new notebook out and smiled at the picture of AstroCat on the cover.

On the first page I wrote:

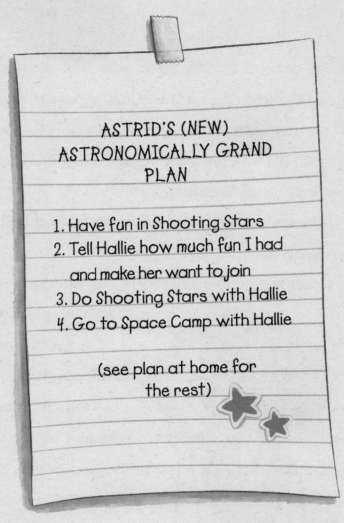

ASTRID'S (NEW)
ASTRONOMICALLY GRAND
PLAN

1. Have fun in Shooting Stars
2. Tell Hallie how much fun I had
   and make her want to join
3. Do Shooting Stars with Hallie
4. Go to Space Camp with Hallie

(see plan at home for
the rest)

Now, I just needed to have fun. Fun that
would make my best friend change her mind.

★ CHAPTER 3 ★

SHOOTING STARS

As I wrote, a boy slid onto the stool next to mine. I hoped he wouldn't get used to that seat—Hallie would need it next time.

A voice at the front said: "Errbod ava ee."

Oops. It was Ms. Ruiz. She was starting. And I'd forgotten to give her the clip-on mic for my hearing aids.

Gripping the pouch the mic was in, I shot my hand up.

But Ms. Ruiz was looking the other way. She was still talking. With her back to me, and with all the noise, I couldn't understand her.

What if she was telling us what to do for an Astro Mission?

I waved my hand back and forth.

Ms. Ruiz finally saw me. "Yes?"

I held out the mic. "Um . . . this is for you."

"Oh, of course." She smiled, took the mic from me, and clicked it on. "Sorry about that! Astrid Peterson, right? Mr. Klein said you're quite a brain at math."

My cheeks warmed. "He did?"

"Yep." She clipped the mic to her jacket. Her nails were painted pink with green

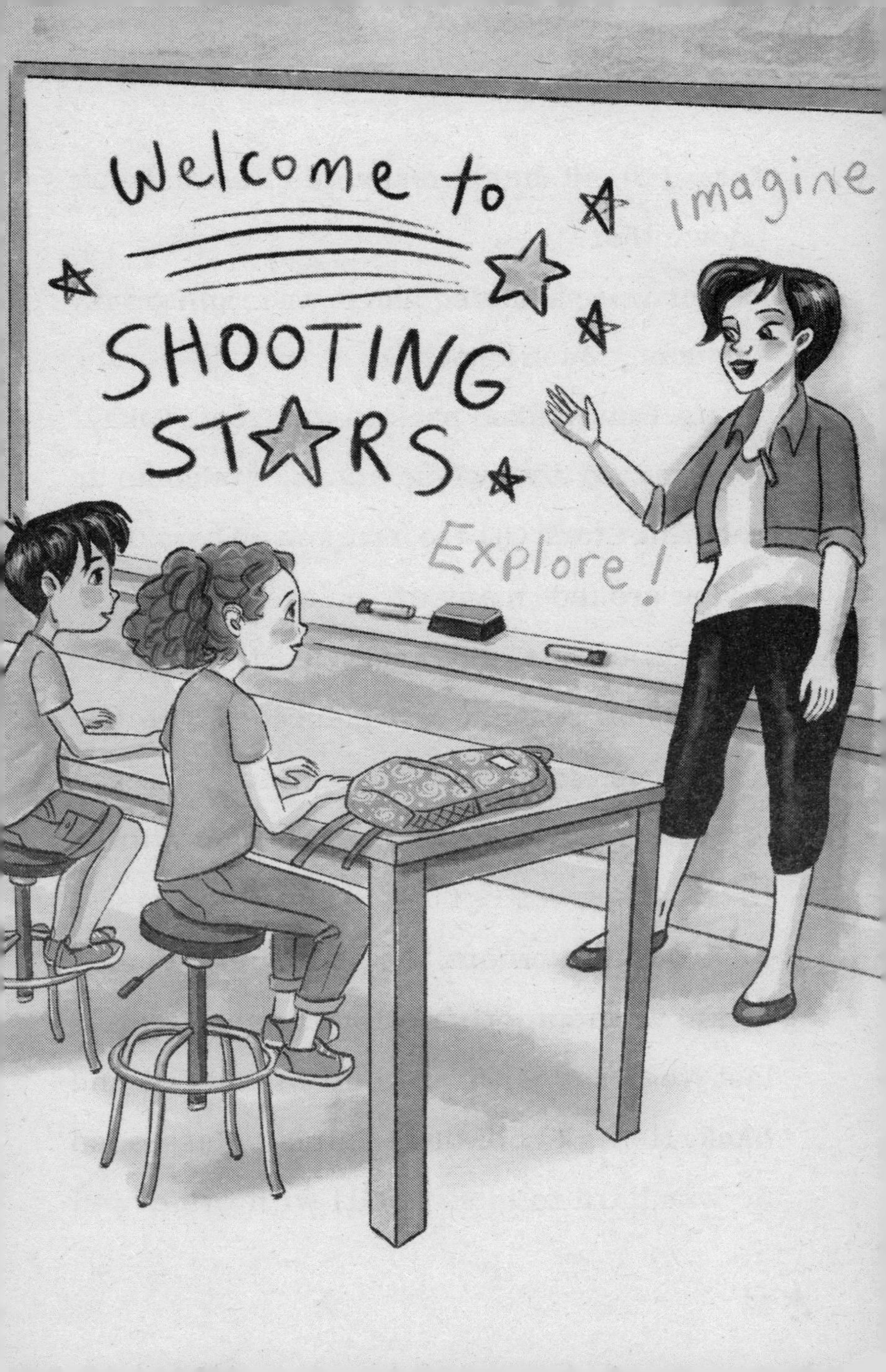

Welcome to
SHOOTING STARS
imagine
Explore!

dots. I liked her already. Ms. Ruiz smiled. "How's that?"

Her voice sounded like it was right on my shoulder. "Much better."

Ms. Ruiz walked back to the front. "Okay," she said to the whole room. "Welcome to Shooting Stars! Glad to have you all here. Take a look around—many of you are future engineers, scientists, and yes, even astronauts!"

I sat up straight and glanced at the boy next to me. Messy hair covered one of his eyes. It didn't make him look much like he wanted to talk to anyone.

Around the room, the other kids seemed to know one another. A boy from my class last year sat with a group of kids at the back. He had cool blue-rimmed glasses, so he was hard to miss. A girl with bright red hair was with them. I'd seen her before too. Another girl wore a real flight jacket.

"Now, as you might know," continued Ms. Ruiz, "every summer I lead a trip to Space Camp. I hope you'll all come. And this year we will be able to offer one full scholarship!"

Hands went up.

"What's a scholarship?" asked a boy.

"That means you don't have to pay," the girl with the flight jacket said.

I gasped. Go to Space Camp . . . for *free*?

My parents didn't want to send me because it cost too much. If I got the scholarship, it would be free. This was my chance!

The boy's eyes got big too. Whispers rose up around the room.

I wasn't the only one who wanted to go for free.

"But first we have a whole year of science-filled fun!" said Ms. Ruiz. "We'll meet twice a week—Mondays and Fridays. We'll have a lot of Astro Missions. These will be projects to help you learn about space and science. You'll do them in teams and earn points from them. They will also help you be good problem-solvers, just like real astronauts."

The girl with the flight jacket raised her hand.

"Yes, Pearl."

"Who gets the scholarship?" Pearl asked, tossing her ponytail.

Ms. Ruiz smiled. "Whoever earns the most points from Astro Missions. Most will be easier and only worth one point. Some will be harder or take longer. Those will be worth as many as five points. For the harder ones, you may earn partial credit. We'll keep track on the Astro Board." She pointed behind her to a poster with a large grid on it. A ton of names were already listed there.

I gulped. There were *so many* names. And only one scholarship. I scanned the list. I found my own name—Astrid Peterson—fast. But I looked and looked. The name Hallie Chen was not there. She really *wasn't* signed up for Shooting Stars.

"Our first Astro Mission is this Friday. It'll be easy—just one point. Before that, I thought a warm-up would be nice." Ms. Ruiz began passing out paper bags. "It's for doing at home. It won't earn you points for the Astro Board, but it might help you in other ways." She waggled her eyebrows like she had a secret.

Chewing my lip, I waited for my bag.

All I had to do was get the max number of points on every Astro Mission. How hard could that be? Ms. Ruiz had said they were problems to solve, and I was good at math.

But what if that wasn't what she'd meant?

One thing was for sure: whatever the Astro Missions were, they would be easier with a friend.

I *had* to get Hallie to change her mind.

★ CHAPTER 4 ★

GUMDROPS AND TOOTHPICKS

That night I sat down at the kitchen table with the bag from Ms. Ruiz. There was a lot of stuff inside, so I dumped it all out to see it better. Gumdrops and toothpicks fell all over the place. A piece of paper flew out. Gumdrops rolled off the table.

Yikes! Maybe dumping hadn't been the best idea.

"Hey, sis." Stella opened the fridge, her tablet tucked under one arm. "What are you doing?"

I slipped under the table to pick up the gumdrops. "Ms. Ruiz gave us homework."

"For Shooting Stars? Oh, fun!" Stella said. "Can I help?"

Yes! I wanted to say. But I bit my lip. "I don't know. That might be against the rules." Ms. Ruiz hadn't said so, but I didn't want to do something wrong so soon. "Don't you have homework?"

"Done." Stella shrugged, putting a milk carton back into the refrigerator. "I'm working on my robot arm."

"Mm," I said. I was reading the piece of paper. Ms. Ruiz wanted us to build different shapes. I set to work on the first one—a square. The gumdrops would be the corners, with the toothpicks pushed in for sides. Easy peasy.

Stella set her tablet and milk glass on the table. "This video has some great ideas," she said. "But I'm missing some of the pieces they use."

"Bummer," I said. I looked at the second shape—a cube. Also easy. I could use my square as the base of it.

"And I don't have the money for new parts." Stella pulled her hair to one side, thinking.

Her hair was straight like Mom's. I'd gotten Dad's curls. Most days I pulled my hair back into a puffy ponytail. Stella used to wear her hair that way too, except for the puffy part. But lately, she'd been wearing it loose.

"Have you asked Mom and Dad?" Pushing the last side into place, I smiled. The cube was perfect. I was rocking Shooting Stars! I flipped the paper over to the last shape. It was a . . . *truncated pyramid*? Huh?

"Mom reminded me they just sent me to Space Camp." Stella took a gulp of milk. "She said I have to use what I have."

There was a diagram on the paper, but it was weird. The shape looked like a flattened cube, but that couldn't be right.

"How am I supposed to build this?" I asked. "Sit on my cube and squish it?"

Stella moved the directions in front of her. "Hmm."

"It doesn't say what to do," I told her.

"Yep." She nodded. "That sounds like Ms. Ruiz."

Stella's tablet buzzed; a text had just come through. She glanced at it, laughed, and typed a reply. She turned back to me. "Look," she said, pointing at the diagram. "It *is* like the cube. But the top square has shorter sides. So just cut some of the toothpicks in half."

I shook my head. "Ms. Ruiz didn't say we could change the materials. That can't be the right way to do it."

Stella shrugged, eyes back on her tablet. "If you say so. I've gotta go."

As she shut our bedroom door down the hall, I sighed. I squinted at the picture. Stella was right; it *did* look like the square at the top had shorter sides than the square at the bottom. But what if I cut the toothpicks and Ms. Ruiz said it was cheating?

Even if this wasn't an Astro Mission, I still had to get it right. I wanted Ms. Ruiz to be impressed. I wanted her to tell Mr. Klein, *Wow, you were right about that Astrid Peterson. What a brain!*

I stashed all the stuff back inside the bag.

I'd just have to keep thinking. After all, Friday was four whole days away.

CHAPTER 5

A GIANT MESS

"So . . . you never said why you aren't doing Shooting Stars," I said. Hallie and I were at lunch the next day, and I was picking at my leftover pasta.

Hallie didn't say anything and took a big bite of her sandwich. Then she pointed to her mouth and shrugged. It was like she was looking for an excuse not to answer.

I tried another angle. "You know, Shooting Stars is going to be sooo fun. Stella said one time they went to a trampoline park. They pretended they were walking on the moon."

"Hmm." Hallie took a sip from her boxed milk. "Do you like my nails? My mom did them." She waved sparkly pink nails at me.

"Ms. Ruiz had pink nails too!" I said. "And the coolest space T-shirt."

"Great," Hallie said. But I think she rolled her eyes while she was scooping up her stuff. "I'm done with my lunch. Want to check out a jump rope?"

I chewed my lip. I wasn't making Shooting Stars sound fun enough. And . . . well . . . it *wasn't* very fun yet. The paper bag assignment sure didn't count. It was at the bottom of my backpack. I still hadn't figured out the last shape. By now, my cube probably *did* look like a truncated pyramid.

☆   ☆   ☆

For the rest of the week, I kept trying with Hallie. We had the first Astro Mission on Friday. I *needed* her. But it was like one of AstroCat's force fields was up. She just kept saying "hmm" or changing the subject.

Finally, it was Friday. I went to the STEM lab by myself.

"So, how did you all do with the shapes?" Ms. Ruiz asked as she clipped on the mic for me. Today, she wore a blue flight suit like the ones astronauts wear. Her nails were neon yellow.

"I did it!" shouted the kid with blue glasses. "See?"

Other kids held up their truncated pyramids too.

"Well done!" declared Ms. Ruiz.

I slid my bag under the table, my cheeks hot. No way was I showing her mine. I'd only done the cube.

A lot of kids had used two toothpicks on each side of the square on the bottom. That made the base bigger. Why hadn't I thought of that?

The boy next to me set his shape onto the table. His top square's toothpicks were short. He'd cut them like Stella had suggested. I sniffed, waiting for Ms. Ruiz to see it. I was

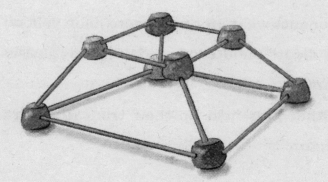

sure she'd tell him he'd done it wrong. But when she walked by our table, all she said was, "Nice work, Veejay!"

Huh.

Well, this wasn't a *real* mission, right? So . . . maybe getting the right answer didn't matter.

Ms. Ruiz stood at the front of the room again. "As you all know, the first Astro Mission is today."

I sat up, folding my hands in front of me. Getting the right answer would matter now.

"All Astro Missions will use skills an astronaut needs to have," said Ms. Ruiz. "Today, you'll be using Morse code—a code that can be used to send messages. Your partner is the person next to you. And don't forget to think outside the box." She winked. "Most problems have more than one solution."

I held my hand up.

"Yes, Astrid?"

"What about people who aren't here today?"

Ms. Ruiz began handing out small boxes. The lids were all closed. "Don't worry," she said. "There will be a lot more Astro Missions."

I bit my lip. Hallie was going to be behind.

Ms. Ruiz set a box on my table.

I took a deep breath. *Think fun,* I told myself.

But the boy next to me—Veejay—grabbed the box.

"Hey," I said. "We're supposed to share that."

"Right. Sorry." He put the box back onto the table. "Is your friend in third grade too?"

"How did you know—?"

"Third graders never get the high scores

40

on the Astro Board. It's like a practice year. A fourth or fifth grader always wins."

"What grade are *you* in?"

"Third."

"Then it's your first year too. So, how do you know that a third grader can't win?"

Still not sharing the box with me, he opened it. "My sister said so. She did Shooting Stars last year. But she gave up; she's doing basketball this year."

I gulped. "Well, Ms. Ruiz didn't say that was a rule." Wait—what if she *had* said that and I just hadn't heard it? Maybe she'd said it before I gave her the clip-on mic.

"It's not official," Veejay said. "It's just the way things happen."

I jutted my chin out. "Then I'll be the first third grader to do it."

"If you say so." He pulled a piece of paper out of the box and began reading it—to himself.

My throat felt thick. Around us, everybody else was bent over their boxes. As partners. Hallie would never act like this kid. She would've shared the box with me. We'd be working together right now.

Finally, I sniffed. "You have to share."

He slid the box an inch closer to me, and I peeked inside. It was filled with pink and green Os—cereal. There were also two pieces of string and two pens.

Or there would've been. Veejay had already taken out one piece of string.

I leaned over him to read the instructions.

Ms. Ruiz hadn't said there was a time limit. But I still wanted to finish first.

I finished reading. "Okay," I said. "So, we

need to spell our names in Morse code with the cereal. The code is on the paper. It's all dots and lines."

"They're called dashes."

"Okay, fine. Dots and dashes. Easy!"

Veejay snorted.

"What's so funny?"

"Astro Missions are never what you think. My sister told me so," he said. "There's always a problem—something you have to figure out on your own. The *real* Astro Mission." He slid a piece of cereal onto his string.

"Well, this seems easy to me." I grabbed a handful of the cereal. "*A* first. *A* for Astrid."

I pulled the paper closer. An *A* in Morse code was a dot and a dash.

The tough part was probably that we didn't have dots and dashes. We just had cereal. We had to pick one color for dots and one for dashes.

Okay, I thought. *Pink for dots, green for dashes.*

So, *A* would be pink, green.

I strung the cereal, then gave Veejay a look that said *I told you so.*

The next letter, *S*, was dot, dot, dot. I put three pinks Os onto my string and grinned. At this rate I really would finish first.

Okay, *T.* Just one dash.

I tapped Veejay's arm. "I need more green, please."

He hunched over the box. "There aren't any more."

I took a deep breath. "Okay. Ms. Ruiz," I called, raising my hand. "We need more green cereal, please."

A couple of kids giggled.

"Astrid has found the *real* challenge here." Ms. Ruiz clapped her hands. "Out in space, astronauts don't always have the things they need. They have to be able to solve problems with what they *do* have." She smiled like she had some great secret.

"Is she serious?" I whispered.

Veejay smirked. Hair flopped in front of his face again. "I tried to tell you."

The girl with the flight jacket—Pearl—raced up to Ms. Ruiz. "We're done." She beamed as she handed Ms. Ruiz a box.

Ms. Ruiz peered inside. "Stellar job!"

I gritted my teeth. This was all Veejay's fault. Maybe there *was* enough green cereal. Maybe he'd just taken all of it for himself.

"Let me see the box!" I demanded. I jerked

it away from him, and cereal spilled all over the floor. Veejay stepped off his stool. *Smush* went the cereal.

"What did you do?" I yelled.

"Me?!" he shouted. "*You* pulled the box."

"If you'd been sharing, I wouldn't have done that."

"Hey, you two, what's going on?" Ms. Ruiz stood behind me, hands on her hips. She was frowning as she took the box away.

I fought back tears. "There isn't enough cereal."

Ms. Ruiz put a hand on my shoulder. "It's okay, Astrid," she said. "We're just about done for today, anyway. There will be an Astro Mission again next Friday. It'll be worth *three points*."

The class gasped.

Ms. Ruiz smiled at me. "You and Veejay can try again then."

I sniffed, staring at the floor.

Veejay had been right. The cereal left in the box had all been pink. Because pink dust now covered the floor.

My first Astro Mission was an astronomical failure.

★ CHAPTER 6 ★

FRIENDS FOR NEVER

Veejay and I spent the rest of the meeting sweeping.

As I dumped the last crumbs into the trash, I peeked inside the other boxes.

Most kids had used the pens; they'd colored half their cereal black. A few had taken bites out of some of the cereal to make it different from the rest.

I hadn't even thought about doing those things. I'd been too busy being mad at Veejay. If I'd been working with Hallie, we would have figured it out.

This partner thing was going to be a problem.

☆　　☆　　☆

After school the next Monday, I finally caught up with Hallie. Shouting kids sped past us, eager to get to clubs. They were loud, and my hearing aids picked up all of it. The noise made it hard to think.

Okay, I told myself. *Fun.*

Hallie was heading for the front of the school again. She held a large brown folder and was walking with a girl I didn't know. The girl said something, and they giggled together.

"Hey, Hallie," I said. I tried to smile, but I was suddenly feeling very small.

She almost dropped the folder. Her cheeks went pink. "Oh . . . hi, Astrid."

Now was the time. I had to tell Hallie how much fun I was having. But instead, I blurted out, "You missed the first Astro Mission."

"Uh . . . I'll see you in there, Hallie," said the girl.

"Okay, Chantal." Hallie turned back to me and frowned. "Astrid, I'm not doing Shooting Stars, remember?"

"But it's . . . *fun*. I thought maybe you'd change your mind," I said. I smiled harder.

Two kids walked past us. They had the same folders as Hallie. "See you there!" they called to her.

"Okay!" She waved back.

I frowned. "Wait . . . where are you going?"

Hallie bit her lip. "Petite Picassos."

"You're going to a different club?"

Hallie nodded. "I'm ... I'm sorry I didn't tell you. I just—you were so excited about Shooting Stars. I know it's been in your Grand Plan for a long time."

I folded my arms. "It's the '*Astronomically* Grand Plan' now, remember? I told you that. And it was *our* plan. You're not going to be ready for Space Camp next summer."

Hallie looked at her shoes. "But ... I don't really want to go."

"Like, ever?" I sputtered. "But ... but we've been planning this since first grade."

"No, *you*'ve been planning it," she said. "It was fun playing space stuff when we were little, and I still like *AstroCat*, but . . ." She shrugged. "Petite Picassos is at the same time as Shooting Stars."

"What is it?"

"It's for art. Right now, we're drawing upside-down pictures." She grinned, pulling a piece of paper out of her folder. "See? It's a woman with a hat." Then she turned the paper upside-down. "And like this, it's a picture of a man. The hat is now the man's collar."

I frowned. "So is it a picture of the man or the woman?"

"It's both! It just depends on how you look at it. Isn't that cool?"

I guessed it was kind of cool. But I wanted to tell her how much cooler *space* was. And how alone I felt last week. I wanted to tell her about the first mission and how it had failed. That I needed a partner I could count on. But the words got stuck in my throat.

"I'm sorry, Astrid," she said, shrugging again. "But Petite Picassos is *so much fun.*"

"But you *have* to do Shooting Stars!" I finally shouted.

"No, I *don't.*"

I stamped my foot. "Well... well, art is boring!"

For a second Hallie didn't say a word. Then she looked like she was going to cry. But she narrowed her eyes instead. "Well, then, we can't be friends anymore!" Hallie stomped down the hallway.

What had I done?

I didn't even mean it—I *liked* art.

And now, not only had I failed my first Astro Mission, but I'd also lost my best friend.

CHAPTER 7

ROBOT JUNKYARD ON THE KITCHEN TABLE

The house smelled like garlic and spices when Mom and I got home from Shooting Stars.

I followed the smell. Dad was stirring a pot in the kitchen. I wrapped my arms around him.

"Hey there, Astrogirl." He hugged me back. "I'm making my famous pasta sauce." He nodded at my sister. "We're going to need the table soon, Stella Bella."

Robot parts covered the table.

"Mm-hmm." Stella frowned, trying to get two pieces apart.

I plopped into the chair across from her. "Is that the robot arm?"

"Yeah." She sighed. "I'm using fewer pieces now. But I'm still having the same problem. I keep running out of this kind." She held up a long, skinny plastic stick. "I just need one more like this, five inches long. Ugh!" She pushed the arm away. "Hey, how was your first Astro Mission?"

Across the kitchen, Dad hummed while he stirred.

"Fine."

Stella raised an eyebrow. "Just 'fine'? The Astrid I know doesn't use words like that to talk about space stuff."

I sighed. "Hallie changed her mind. She doesn't want to join."

"Oh no!" Stella said. "You guys have been planning this for forever."

"For one year and eleven months," I said. "But I'm still trying to talk her into doing it. Once I tell her how fun it is, I'm sure she'll quit Petite Picassos."

"Hmm."

"So far, I've been working with this other kid—Veejay. But I don't think he wants to work with me very much."

Stella squinted at her robot arm. "Well, what's your backup plan?"

"What?"

She sifted through a pile of loose tiny parts. "Hallie might not change her mind, right? So, what will you do if she doesn't?"

"It's *always* been Hallie and me," I said. "It's in the Astronomically Grand Plan. I can't make it through the next Astro Mission without her. Ms. Ruiz said it would be a tough one."

"Two points?"

"Three."

"Yikes!" Stella pushed a tiny piece into the arm. "But you'll be fine, Astrid. Sometimes, to get what you want, you have to change."

I thought about the ways Stella had changed. She loved robots now. She was always texting her friends. She went to a different school. And she wore her hair down instead of in a ponytail. But we were still sisters. She still loved me. Maybe *that* would never change.

"Think about it like a scientist," she continued. "The problem is that you need a friend, right? Well, it's like Ms. Ruiz always says: most problems have more than one solution."

"Like I could make friends with Veejay instead?"

"Or both Veejay *and* Hallie." Stella tried to force a different piece in. "This is never going to fit! I'm going to have to buy new parts!"

I thought about what Stella had said. I studied the robot arm, then picked up two short pieces.

"That won't work," she said.

But I stuck them together. Then I pulled a hair tie off Stella's wrist. I wrapped it around them. Then I put the piece in place. "Well, maybe there's more than one solution."

Stella's eyes lit up. She attached the ends. Then she moved the other parts of the robotic arm. "You did it!"

I grinned as she made the arm pat my head.

Maybe Stella was right. I didn't have any friends in Shooting Stars. Neither did Veejay. But he also didn't seem like he *wanted* any. I didn't know if we could start over, but I could try.

And what about Hallie? I'd almost made her cry. My stomach felt bad just thinking about it. I had to tell her I was sorry. But . . . we'd *always* done space-y stuff together. Could we still be friends if we liked different things now?

I twisted a few scraps of Stella's wires. The blue and purple looked pretty together.

And then an idea popped into my head. "Hey, can I have these?" I asked Stella.

"Sure," she said. She scooped the other parts into a box. "Less for me to clean up!"

I raced back to our room, ready to put my plan into action.

· CHAPTER 8 ·

THE REAL ASTRO MISSION

On Friday I tried to catch Hallie after school, but she was already gone. I'd tried to catch her every day this week. But she'd been out sick Tuesday. And after that, she'd been hanging out with kids from Petite Picassos, and I didn't want to talk to her with other people around.

I bit my lip. I guessed I'd find her later.

Anyway, I wanted to get to Shooting Stars

early. Veejay and I had to get this Astro Mission right.

But when I got to the STEM lab, I skidded to a halt. The door was closed. Kids stood outside. Had Shooting Stars been canceled today?

I found Veejay. "Do you know what's going on?"

He shook his head. "No, but I saw Ms. Ruiz inside. She's wearing her flight suit. I think she's setting up."

I gulped. "This Astro Mission must be a hard one."

"It *is* worth three points."

I nodded. Then I took a deep breath. "I'm sorry about last time," I said. "And I'm sorry I grabbed the cereal."

"Me too," he said. "I mean, I'm sorry I didn't share with you. I . . . I like working by myself.

I'm used to it. But I promise I'll share this time."

I smiled. "I'd like that."

Finally, Ms. Ruiz opened the door. But she put a hand up to stop us from going in.

She grinned. "Welcome to your first three-point Astro Mission!"

I wiggled to the front of the crowd. I switched on the mic, and Ms. Ruiz clipped it to her collar.

Now her voice boomed into my ears: "Everyone, find a partner."

Veejay scooted up next to me. I nodded back to him.

"Good," Ms. Ruiz said as everyone else paired up. "Today's mission has to do with teamwork. Astronauts must use teamwork to fix things that break. And things don't always go as planned. Today, one partner will go inside. They will be mission control. The other will stay out here. They are the astronaut. My friend, Mr. Lipton, will watch the astronauts. But you astronauts will still have to do the work yourselves, working with mission control."

Mr. Lipton waved, then put his nose back in a book.

"Each pair may talk to each other using walkie-talkies." Ms. Ruiz passed a small brown box to one person in each pair. When she got to us, she handed the box to me and winked. Then she announced, "If I just gave you a box, you're the astronaut."

I raised an eyebrow at Veejay. He shrugged back.

"Inside the lab there is an engine part,"

said Ms. Ruiz. "The astronauts won't be able to see it. The partners—mission control—will need to tell their astronauts what it looks like. The astronauts will then build the same part, outside at the table. There are only two rules. One: the astronauts are not allowed to see the engine part inside. And two: no one may leave or enter the classroom."

My smile faded. We had to build *engine parts*?

"Talk with your partner while I hand these out. Make sure to come up with backup plans." Ms. Ruiz handed each of us a pair of walkie-talkies. She pointed to a large, gray square on the side of one of them. "Remember to press this button while you talk. Then say 'over' so the other person knows you're done talking."

I frowned. "This sounds really hard."

"Yeah." Veejay's brow wrinkled.

I shook my head. "You don't get it. I won't be able to understand you. My hearing aids help, but I need to see your face, too."

"We can do that." Veejay pointed. "We can use the window. I can take peeks at the engine part, then talk to you through the walkie-talkie while I'm looking at you." He frowned. "Why do you think she wants us to have a backup plan?"

"Maybe it's like you said. There's always going to be a problem. The *real* Astro Mission."

"Time to go in," Ms. Ruiz told half of us. Her smile was way too big.

"Here goes nothing," Veejay said.

As soon as our partners were inside, the rest of us hurried around the corner. Mr. Lipton leaned against a pole. He barely looked up from his book.

Ms. Ruiz had set up a table for us to work on. A black curtain hung on a rod in front of the table. Our partners inside wouldn't be able to see our engine parts. And we wouldn't be able to see the one we were trying to copy.

I opened my box.

It was filled with gumdrops of all colors. And a bag of toothpicks too.

"Ha!" I said. "Just like the practice mission!"

Next to me, Pearl opened her box and pouted. "How are we supposed to build an engine part out of gumdrops?"

My walkie-talkie hissed. "Come in, Astrid. Over."

I held down the button like Ms. Ruiz had shown us. "Veejay? Can you hear me?"

Veejay waved from the window. "You're supposed to say 'over.'"

"Sorry. Over."

"And yes, I can hear you. Over." Behind Veejay, kids crowded around a desk. A curtain, like ours, hung in front of it. From where the astronauts were, we couldn't see what they were looking at.

"What's the engine part made out of?" I asked Veejay. "Um . . . over."

He grinned. "Gumdrops and toothpicks. Over."

"Phew! That's what I have in my box." I laughed. Maybe this wouldn't be so bad after all. "What shape is it? Over." When I looked up, Veejay was shaking his walkie-talkie and frowning. I pressed the button on mine. "What's wrong? Over."

I held it up to listen.

He shook it again, but it did no good. He

pulled Ms. Ruiz over. He pointed to the walkie-talkie. Another inside kid came over to her too, pointing at hers. But Ms. Ruiz just smiled and shrugged.

A boy next to me shook his walkie-talkie. "Hey! Is yours working?" he asked.

My shoulders sagged. The walkie-talkies were *supposed* to break. Just like with the truncated pyramid and the Morse code project—there was something wrong with what we were given. And Ms. Ruiz wasn't going to fix it for us. *We* were supposed to figure out what to do. To think "outside the box." Just like Veejay and my sister had both said.

This was the *real* Astro Mission.

★ CHAPTER 9 ★

RIGHT ANSWER

I collapsed onto a bench. What should we do?

If we knew American Sign Language, it would have been easy. I knew the alphabet, but that was about it. And Veejay probably didn't even know that. I'd have to teach it to him sometime. But what were we going to do today?

Around me, kids were freaking out. Pearl

bit her nails. One boy had run up to the window, waving his arms. Another girl just kept shouting, "It's not working!"

And then I thought of something. Maybe Petite Picassos had the right idea. Like Hallie's upside-down art, we needed to think about this problem in a different way.

One time, the batteries in my hearing aids died in the middle of school. I'd searched my bag, but I didn't have any new ones. I couldn't hear anybody. It was a really bad day.

It was like that now, but for all of us.

And suddenly, I knew what to do.

I knocked on the window to get Veejay's attention.

He raised his arms in the air, as if saying, *What can we do?*

I pointed to my hearing aids. Then I made

an oval with my fingers. I pretended I was talking into it. I pointed at Ms. Ruiz.

Veejay's eyes got big and he grinned. He ran back to Ms. Ruiz, but she didn't have the mic anymore. Veejay was smart, though. He ran back to her desk.

Next to me, Pearl frowned. "What are you guys doing?"

Veejay was at the window again. He was talking into the clip-on mic, but I couldn't hear him. By now, all the kids outside had crowded around me. I tapped on the window and pointed for Veejay to turn on the mic.

He did it. "Hello? Astrid?"

I grinned and nodded. "I can hear you!"

A few kids outside cheered.

But Pearl crossed her arms. "That's cheating."

I bit my lip. "Ms. Ruiz told us the rules. She never said we couldn't use my clip-on mic."

"Well, it's not fair!"

"Don't be mean, Pearl," said the boy with blue glasses.

I scanned the kids behind me. They wanted that scholarship too.

"Let's all work together," I said. "No more teams. That's what real astronauts would do, anyway, right?"

"Yeah!" shouted a couple of kids.

"Oh, I'm in." The boy with blue glasses grinned. "I'm Dominic, by the way."

"I'm Astrid," I said. "Nice to meet you."

Pearl's nose twitched. "I still think you're breaking the rules."

"Are you in or out?" Dominic asked.

"Out," she huffed. "Noa and I will find the *right* answer."

She stomped away from the group, and I was worried. What if there *was* a better answer?

"What's he saying, Astrid?" asked a kid behind me.

I turned back to Veejay. By now, everyone inside was gathered around him too. Except Noa, who was trying to talk to Pearl.

The clip-on mic wasn't the same as a walkie-talkie. It was only one-way. I could hear Veejay, but he couldn't hear me. I moved my hand in a circle, hoping to show that we were all a team now.

Veejay gave a thumbs-up. "We'll work together inside, too."

"He says we're all going to work together," I told the group outside.

They cheered.

Dominic sat at the table. "Ask him what shape the ... um ... engine part is."

I fit my hands together and mouthed "shape" to Veejay.

"Oh, *shape*?" said Veejay. "It's a cube."

The red-haired girl grabbed the mic from Veejay. "Hi, I'm Ella. The gumdrops are the corners; the toothpicks are the sides." She passed the mic back.

"Okay," he said. "On the bottom of the cube, there are two purple gumdrops and two white ones." A boy whispered to him, and Veejay added, "The purples are next to each other. So are the white ones."

I passed this on to the crowd behind me.

They helped Dominic make the square. Then they put in toothpicks, sticking up, ready for the colors on top. I gave a thumbs-up back to Veejay.

"Okay, the four colors on the top are . . ." He turned to listen to a kid behind him. "Two black and two red."

"Two black, two red," I repeated.

"Wait, which are which?" Dominic asked.

I held my hands out to Veejay and bit my lip.

He and Ella were arguing.

Mr. Lipton turned the page in his book and yawned.

Next to me, Pearl darted between the table and the window. Her cube was hidden inside her box. She and Noa seemed to be using a code to talk.

Dominic came up behind me. He waved

his hands to get Veejay's and Ella's attention. He had two other kids make a cube with their hands. Then he pointed to one of the top corners.

Veejay and Ella fought for the mic.

"Oh, I get it!" said Veejay. "That one is black."

"Black," I said for Dominic.

We went through the other three, one by one. It was four thirty p.m. Almost time to go home.

As if she'd read my mind, Ms. Ruiz called, "Okay, astronauts! Time to come home!"

"You're all going to fail," Pearl hissed.

Dominic held up our model like it was a work of art.

I giggled. Ella rolled her eyes from the window, but she was smiling too. Next to her, Veejay was doing a victory dance.

And walking inside with my brand-new friends, it was easy to pretend I hadn't heard Pearl. I couldn't be anything but happy.

★ CHAPTER 10 ★

MY NEW PLAN

"Let's see what you've got!" Ms. Ruiz called.

We stood around the table, and she pulled back the curtain. I checked all the gumdrops. Our cube was an exact copy. We'd done it!

"Yes!" I shouted.

Dominic pumped his fist. Other kids cheered.

Pearl pursed her lips. Her cube had pink gumdrops instead of red. Everything else was right, though.

Ms. Ruiz frowned. "I see Dominic's and Pearl's models. But where are the others?"

Dominic nodded at me, wanting me to tell her.

My cheeks got hot as everybody turned to look at me. This had been all my idea. If Pearl was right, and everyone failed the Astro Mission, it would be my fault.

"Well, our walkie-talkies broke," I told Ms. Ruiz. I tried not to let my voice shake. "*Nobody's* worked. But my clip-on mic—the one I give you to wear—was already in mission control, so I told Veejay to use it. Then we decided to work as a big team. It wouldn't have been fair otherwise."

Ms. Ruiz raised her eyebrows. "And did you all agree to this?"

Everybody except Pearl and Noa nodded.

Ms. Ruiz's eyes twinkled. "That was fast thinking, Astrid. You know, I've led Shooting Stars for a long time. We've done this mission before. I've never had an entire class work together. And you copied the cube perfectly, too. Your team gets the full three points!"

We all cheered.

"Pearl, Noa, what did the two of you decide?"

"Noa and I made our own model," Pearl said. "We used Morse code to talk. And she pointed to things for the colors. But we didn't get it all right."

"It was still a good idea," said Ms. Ruiz. "And you were very close. Two points each."

Noa shrugged. Pearl folded her arms.

Ms. Ruiz walked to the Astro Board just as the bell rang. "See you next time!" she called to everyone.

Kids ran to get their backpacks and clean up.

Pearl came up to me. "I guess maybe you had the right answer after all."

I blinked. "No, I didn't. I just had *one* of them. There's more than one way to solve a problem, remember? You did great too."

"Well . . . thanks," she said.

Veejay tapped my shoulder as Pearl went to get her backpack.

"We did it!" he whispered. We grinned and high-fived.

We'd beaten our first three-point Astro Mission!

Space Camp felt closer than ever.

☆ ☆ ☆

After Shooting Stars, I found Hallie at the front of the school. It was finally just the two of us. I held the bracelet I'd made behind my back. "Hey," I said.

She frowned. "Oh. Hi."

"I—I'm sorry," I said. "I didn't even know

you liked art so much. I should have listened to what you wanted."

Hallie looked down. "I'm sorry I didn't tell you sooner. I know you love space stuff."

"And art isn't boring," I said quickly. "Actually, your upside-down art helped me think during the Astro Mission today."

"Really?"

I nodded. "It's like what Ms. Ruiz says: most problems have more than one solution." I held my hand out. "I made you something. It's art and science—together."

Hallie took the bracelet. I'd threaded beads onto the blue and purple wires—some were black and some were pink. Stella had found them for me in her junk piles. "Ooo, this is pretty," Hallie breathed. "But . . . um . . . how is it science-y?"

"It says 'friends forever' in Morse code," I said. I showed her the bracelet I was wearing. They were the same. "See?"

"Cool!" She fingered the bracelet.

"Friends?" I asked.

She grinned. "Friends *forever.*"

☆   ☆   ☆

After Hallie was picked up, I took out my AstroCat notebook and sat down on a bench. It was time to update the plan again.

ASTRID'S (NEW) ASTRONOMICALLY GRAND PLAN

1. Have fun in Shooting Stars
2. ~~Tell Hallie how much fun I had and make her want to join~~
3. ~~Do Shooting Stars with Hallie~~
4. Go to Space Camp with ~~Hallie~~ my new friends in Shooting Stars
5. Learn lots of science and math
6. Go to college
7. Go to astronaut training
8. Be an astronaut

Hallie and I could still be friends. I would miss her in Shooting Stars, but she could like art and I could like space. And I decided it was good to leave in the part about having fun. Shooting Stars *was* fun.

Veejay sat down next to me. "What's that?"

"My Astronomically Grand Plan," I said. "For now. I might still need to change it as I get older. There's probably more than one way to get to the last step."

He nodded as he read it. "That's a good plan."

Dad's car pulled up, so I put away the notebook.

"I'm glad you're in Shooting Stars," said Veejay.

"Thanks. I'm glad you are too."

"Partners next time?"

I laughed. "That would be astronomically great."

AUTHOR'S NOTE

I'm an audiologist who supports access to language—whether it be spoken, signed, or both. I've written Astrid with hearing aids and spoken language because I'm the most familiar with that perspective, but I have great respect for the Deaf community and signed languages like American Sign Language (ASL). There are a lot of great books out there with deaf/hard-of-hearing characters that are written from other perspectives. For a starter list, find my profile on Instagram @rienealwriter.

ACKNOWLEDGMENTS

First of all, thank you to YOU, Astrid's readers! I hope this book inspires you to reach for the stars.

As Astrid learns, things just don't work unless you find your team. I am very grateful to have the amazing Carrie Pestritto as my agent. It honestly would not have occurred to me to write an original chapter book series without her guidance. Thank you also to my wonderful editor, Alyson Heller, who saw exactly what I was trying to do with Astrid and loved her from the beginning—and to all the people at Aladdin and Simon & Schuster who made this book into a reality. I'm so honored to get to work with you all.

Many thanks to Danielle Kelsay, Diane Niebuhr, Stephanie Fleckenstein, and everyone else at the University of Iowa Au.D. program, for my education in audiology. Thank you to all the hospitals, clinics, schools, and other places that harbored me as an intern and to all the clients who inspired me along the way. (And special thanks to Amanda Baum, who helped a ton with drummer info for my last project and whom I wasn't able to thank properly then.)

I wouldn't have gotten this far without Leira K. Lewis, Victoria Kazarian, Rosanna Griffin, and Rebecca Cuadra George. Whispering Platypodes forever! Thank you also to SCBWI. And a million warm fuzzies to Teresa Richards, who brought me up to speed on publishing when I started writing and remains the best critique partner ever.

Finally, super big thanks to JMac and SL for putting up with their mom being sucked into pretend worlds all the time. Thank you to my parents for all their love and support. Thank you to Grammy & Pa, for all the visits to NASA Ames over the years. And thank you to Brian, who supported my writing from the beginning. I love you and would not be here without you. Finally, thank you to God for this opportunity.